FLAMINGOS ON THE ROOF

POEMS and PAINTINGS

BY

CALEF BROWN

Houghton Mifflin Company
Boston

For Cara Brodbin and Siddarth Kumar

www.houghtonmifflinbooks.com

The text of this book is set in 16/25-point Calef Bold.
The illustrations were done in acrylic.

Library of Congress Cataloging-in-Publication Data

Brown, Calef.
Flamingos on the roof / written and illustrated by Calef Brown.
p. cm.
ISBN 0-618-56298-2 (hardcover)
1. Children's poetry, American. I. Title.
PS3552.R68525F57 2006
811'.54 c22
2004025125

ISBN-13: 978-0618-56298-5
ISBN-10: 0-618-56298-2

Printed in United States of America
WOZ 10 9 8 7 6 5 4 3 2

CONTENTS

ALPHABET SHERBET

Alphabet Sherbet.
Have you ever heard of it?
   I bought myself a gallon,
   and ate about a third of it.
The A's are all amazing.
   The B's are a beautiful blue.
The C's and D's
are cool and delicious.
   The E's are enjoyable too.
The F's are fair,
but don't you fret—
   the G's are great,
   so go and get
   a bowl of Alphabet Sherbet.
You'll love it,
I'm sure of it!

COMBO TANGO

Dance lesson number one:
   The Combination Tango.
   Listen to the lingo.
This is how the steps go:

Boogie to the banjo.
Bop to the bongo.
   Freeze like an igloo.
   Stomp like a buffalo.
Drop like a yo-yo.
Swing like a golf pro.
   Flip like a hairdo.
   Tumble like a domino.
Swivel on your kneecap.
Wobble like a mud flap.
Take a little catnap.
   Do it all again!

ANGUS

Angus dressed as best he could,
but all his clothes were gray.
     Either that or olive drab,
     the colors of the day.
So Angus sewed a snazzy suit,
with better brighter cloth.
     Not half bad.
     Completely plaid.
He never takes it off.

Flamingos on the Roof

Shortly after midnight
On December twenty-third,
I know it sounds absurd,
but this is what I heard . . .
Flamingos on the roof.
That's the honest truth.
I'm sure I wasn't dreaming,
though I don't have any proof.
I woke my sister Mindy.
We scampered up the chimney.
The night was dark and windy.
Flamingos on the roof.

BOB

Bob the burly biker
built a chopper in a bottle.
No one ever put together
such a perfect model.
All inside a bottle.
So exact, in fact,
it has a throttle
on the side.
Bobby often wishes
he could take it for a ride.

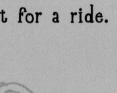

WEATHERBEE'S DINER

Whenever you're looking for something to eat,
Weatherbee's Diner is just down the street.
    Start off your meal with a bottle of rain.
    Fog on the glass is imported from Maine.
The thunder is wonderful, order it loud,
with sun-dried tornado on top of a cloud.
    Snow Flurry Curry is also a treat.
    It's loaded with lightning and slathered in sleet.
Cyclones with hailstones are great for dessert,
but have only one or your belly will hurt.
    Regardless of whether it's chilly or warm,
    at Weatherbee's Diner they cook up a storm!

Bug Show

A pair of mosquitos
   in matching tuxedos
   are happily hosting a show.
Performers come and go.
   Crickets and slugs
   and various bugs
   applaud from down below.
How do slugs applaud, you ask?
   Does anybody know?
Perhaps they tap their shiny tails
   and wag them to and fro.

TEN-CENT HAIKU

I sat down to write a haiku.
It seemed like the right thing to do.
I wouldn't need very much time.
   No need to bother
    with making it rhyme.
I reached in my pocket
   and pulled out a dime.
This is my ten-cent haiku:

Shiny silver friend.
   I will never let you go.
     Look! An ice cream truck!

SALLY

Meet Medusa's sister Sally.
Oh, for goodness sake!
Instead of having hair,
she has a single lazy snake.
If you happen to glance
at Medusa by chance,
you turn to solid rock.
Sally's curse is even worse—
she makes you stop and talk.

BISCUITS IN THE WIND

The latest song from long ago
is "Biscuits in the Wind."
First made famous yesterday
by Andy Mandolin:

My oh my, the years go by,
I wonder where they've been?
Gone astray, or so they say,
like Biscuits in the Wind.

BiRThDaY LighTS

Light bulbs on a birthday cake.
What a difference that would make!
   Plug it in and make a wish,
   then relax and flip the switch!
No more smoke
   or waxy mess
   to bother any birthday guests.
But Grampa says, "It's not the same!
   Where's the magic?
   Where's the flame?
To get your wish without a doubt,
you need to blow some candles out!"

PEAS

Peas peek out of the pod.
   They ponder.
   They whisper.
   They nod.
Everything is new.
   The sky is a dazzling blue.
The wind is in the willow trees.
The sun is on the sod.
   Peas peek out of the pod.

the CRYSTAL BOWLING BALL

Step right up!
  Come one, come all!
  See the Crystal Bowling Ball!
It knows how all the pins will fall
    in all the frames
    of all the games
    on all the lanes
    in every town.
Bowlers come
from miles around.
    They run.
    They walk.
    They even crawl.
They seek the Crystal Bowling Ball.

NEW UTENSIL

I eat my beans with lots of lard.
(The kind without the pork.)
    But here's the rub—
    this tasty grub
    just slides right off my fork.
So . . .
    I found a little ladle
    and a handle from a hatchet.
Several feet of wire
    were required
    to attach it.
For eating slippery lima beans,
    nothing else can match it!

SOGGY CIRCUS

The circus was flooded.
It happened so suddenly.
    What would they do?
    Nobody knew.
The ringmaster shouted,
"It's part of the act!"
    Some of the spectators
    started to boo.
A clown got some laughs
with his kicking and splashing.
    The audience followed his cue.
The strongman just played
with a toy that he made—
    a green origami canoe.

EighT-TreeS

Eight-trees.
Have you seen these?
They grow in several states.
The leaves are shaped like eights.
Make a note to pick a few
and pin them to your skates
to guard against mistakes
when doing figure eights.

MARTIAN MEN

Grandmother Pennybaker
   counted up to ten.
The clock struck eleven
   as she picked up a pen
and sketched out a dozen little Martian men.
   Three,
   then four,
   then five.

Grandfather Pennybaker
   tidied up the den.
The clock struck midnight,
   and he wondered, then,
who drew the funny little Martian men.
   Three,
   then four,
   then five.

the APPLETON TWINS

The Appleton Twins
are a curious pair.
    They never agree,
    but they don't seem to care.
If one of them whispers,
    the other one shouts.
If one of them giggles,
    the other one pouts.
If one of them hushes,
    the other one howls.
If one of them chuckles,
    the other one growls.
If one of them grumbles,
    the other one grins.
Together forever,
the Appleton Twins.

TV TAXi

Television Taxicab.
What a way to travel!
Watch your favorite station
    in Tahiti or Seattle.
What could be more simple?
You can sample every channel.
    Seven, for example,
    features movies (for a fee).
Never mind the passing sights—
    there's nothing much to see.

ALLICATTER GATORPILLAR

Allicatter Gatorpillar
chews a leaf,
shows his teeth.
Allicatter Gatorpillar
sings a song,
then he's gone.
Allicatter Gatorpillar
by and by,
my oh my!
Allibutter Gatorfly!

KiNG of the TiRE

Presenting the King of the Tire.
Remember to call him "sire."
His Majesty's crown
is a tattered old hat.
His calico cat
is a bit of a brat.
Before he retired
he lived in a flat.
But that
was long ago.

BOSSY CASEY

Bossy Casey
   gives advice.
Completely free
   and worth the price.
She reads a list,
   to be precise,
of things you shouldn't do.
   These are just a few:

Never climb a rubber ladder.
   Never punch a kettle.
Never tease a caterpillar.
   Never kiss a nettle.
Never eat the turkey feet,
   but always order fries.
Casey may be bossy,
   but her words are very wise.

POSEIDON'S HAIR

Poseidon's head was nearly bald,
    much to his dismay.
He picked some kelp,
    and with some help,
    he made his own toupee.
Although it smells of oyster shells
    and often floats away,
old Poseidon loves his hair—
    he wears it every day.

WORMS

The worm in the apple
   likes mangos.
The worm in the mango
   likes yams.
The worm in the beet
   likes anything sweet,
   especially jellies and jams.
The worm in the onion
   likes cabbage.
The worm in the cabbage
   likes cheese.
The worm in the pear
   likes a day at the fair.
The worm in the turnip agrees.

ORCHIDS

Orchids are awesome.
Incredibly so.
They steadily grow
deep in the forest
where the tourists
and the florists
never go.

A Camping Tale

I picked a spot to pitch the tent,
and started up a campfire.
   Evening fell,
   and all was well . . .
   until I saw a vampire!
Thinking fast, I hollered "Halt!"
and grabbed a jar of garlic salt.
I shook it in the campfire smoke,
which quickly made the vampire choke.
   He stamped his feet.
   He shook his cloak.
I tried to calm the batty bloke,
and offered him some food.
   The things he said
   before he fled
were really rather rude.

Ray's House

Ray built a house on his nose.
Just for a lark, I suppose.
The lark is content there.
It even pays rent there,
and shovels the stoop when it snows.

BARNACLE BUILT FOR TWO

Life is a dream
with a nautical theme
in a barnacle built for two.
   Stuck on the hull of a sailing ship
   with powerful barnacle glue.
Together we go
with the ebb and the flow
across the ocean blue.
   Hitching a ride on a sailing ship
   in a barnacle built for two.

TINY BABY SPHINX

Tiny Baby Sphinx.
She looks at me and blinks.
I offer bits of cat food,
the kind that really stinks.
I wonder what she thinks about
at nighttime when she slinks about,
inviting other sphinxes out
to gather in the moonlight.